D_ar Parents,

Congratulations! Your child has embarked on an exciting journey – they're learning to read! As a parent, you can be there to support and cheer them along as they take their first steps.

At school, children are taught how to decode words and arrange these building blocks of language into sentences and wonderful stories.

At home, parents play a vital part in reinforcing these new-found skills. You can help your child practise their reading by providing well-written, engaging stories, which you can enjoy together.

This series – **Ready, Steady, Read!** – offers exactly that, and more. These stories support inexperienced readers by:

- gradually introducing new vocabulary
- using repetition to consolidate learning
- gradually increasing sentence length and word count
- providing texts that boost a young reader's confidence.

As each book is completed, engaging activities encourage young readers to look back at the story, while a Picture Dictionary reinforces new vocabulary. Enjoyment is the key – and reading together can be great fun for both parent and child!

Prue Goodwin
Lecturer in Lite

The **Ready, Steady, Read!** series has 4 levels. The facing page shows what you can expect to find in the books at each level.

As your child's confidence grows, they can progress to books from the higher levels. These will keep them engaged and encourage new reading skills.

The levels are only meant as guides; together, you and your child can pick the book that will be just right.

Here are some handy tips for helping children who are ready for reading!

Give them choice – Letting children pick a book (from the level that's right for them) makes them feel involved.

Talk about it – Discussing the story and the pictures helps children engage with the book.

Read it again – Repetition of favourite stories reinforces learning.

Cheer them on! – Praise and encouragement builds a child's confidence and the belief in their growing ability.

LEVEL **1** For first readers

* short, straightforward sentences
* basic, fun vocabulary
* simple, easy-to-follow stories of up to 100 words
* large print and easy-to-read design

LEVEL **2** For developing readers

* longer sentences
* simple vocabulary, introducing new words
* longer stories of up to 200 words
* bold design, to capture readers' interest

LEVEL **3** For more confident readers

* longer sentences with varied structure
* wider vocabulary
* high-interest stories of up to 300 words
* smaller print for experienced readers

LEVEL **4** For able readers

* longer sentences with complex structure
* rich, exciting vocabulary
* complex stories of up to 400 words
* emphasis on text more than illustrations

Once you have read the story, you will find some amazing activities at the back of the book! There are Excellent Exercises for you to complete, plus a super Picture Dictionary.

But first it is time for the story . . .

Ready?

Steady?

Let's read!

Michael Coleman   Gwyneth Williamson

LAZY OZZIE

LITTLE TIGER PRESS
London

Ozzie was lazy.

"It's time you learned to fly," said
Mother Owl sternly. "I want to see
you on the ground when I get back!"

Ozzie thought hard.
Suddenly he noticed a
tall horse just below him.
Ozzie had an idea . . .

"Help, help! It's an emergency!"
he yelled, jumping onto the
high horse. "Take me to
the cowshed!"

So the horse took Ozzie to
the cowshed.

"Emergency!" cried Ozzie, jumping
onto a not-quite-so-high cow.
"Take me to the pigsty!"

So the horse and the cow took
Ozzie to the pigsty.

"Emergency!" cried Ozzie, jumping onto a big pig. "Take me to the farmyard!"

So the horse, the cow
and the pig took Ozzie
to the farmyard.

"Emergency!" cried
Ozzie, jumping onto
a short sheepdog.
"Take me to the field!"

So the horse, the cow,
the pig and the sheepdog
took Ozzie to the field.

"Emergency!" cried Ozzie,
jumping onto a lamb's back.
"Take me to the duck pond!"

So the horse, the cow, the pig,
the sheepdog and the lamb took
Ozzie to the duck pond.

"Emergency!" cried Ozzie,
jumping onto a diddy duck.
"Take me to the barn!"

So the horse, the cow, the pig,
the sheepdog, the lamb and
the duck took Ozzie back
to the barn . . .

Ozzie hopped down to the ground.
He'd done it!

"So where's the emergency?" asked the horse.

"I was only joking!" said Ozzie. "What a hoot, eh?"

The other animals were not amused.

"I flew all the way down," Ozzie said
to Mother Owl when she came back.
But Mother Owl . . .

. . . had been watching all the time.

"So now you can fly back up again," she said!

Excellent Exercises

Have you read the story? Well done!
Now it is time for more fun!

Here are some questions about the story. Ask an adult to
listen to your answers, and help if you get stuck.

Cheeky Chap

This story is all about a cheeky owl who tries to trick
his mother. Have *you* ever tried to trick anyone?
What did you do?

Fun Farm

Can you name all the farm animals in this picture? If you
could catch a ride on any animal, which would you choose?

Horsing About

Now describe what Ozzie is doing in this picture.

Clever Mum

Can you remember what Mother Owl asks Ozzie to do at the end of the story?

Picture Dictionary

Can you read all of these words from the story?

barn

cow

duck

field

horse

jumping

lamb

owl

pig

sheepdog

Can you think of any other words that describe these pictures – for example, what colours can you see? Why not try to spell some of these words? Ask an adult to help!

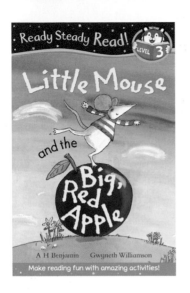

Little Mouse and the Big Red Apple

Mouse does not want to share his big, juicy apple but he is too small to move it on his own. Can he get his friends to help and still eat it all himself?

Nobody Laughs at a Lion!

"I'm the King of the Jungle because I'm the best!" says Pa Lion. But each time he shows off his skills, the other animals start to giggle. Don't they know that NOBODY laughs at a lion?

Ridiculous!

One snowy day, Shelley leaves her cosy bed to go on an adventure. But whoever heard of a tortoise out in winter . . . ? *Ridiculous!*

Who's Been Eating My Porridge?

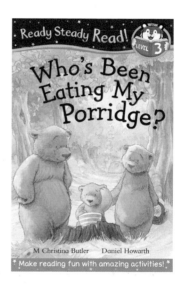

Little Bear will not eat his porridge. So his mother gives it to Old Scary Bear in the woods. Little Bear does not believe in the Scary Bear. But *someone* has been eating his porridge . . . !

In memory of Michael Murphy – M C
For Mum and Dad – G W

LITTLE TIGER PRESS, 1 The Coda Centre, 189 Munster Road, London SW6 6AW
First published in Great Britain 1994
This edition published 2013
Text copyright © Michael Coleman 1994, 2013
Illustrations copyright © Gwyneth Williamson 1994, 2013
All rights reserved
Printed in China
978-1-84895-668-1
LTP/1800/0596/0413
2 4 6 8 10 9 7 5 3 1

Books in the Series

LEVEL 1 - For first readers

LEVEL 2 - For developing readers

LEVEL 3 - For more confident readers

LEVEL 4 - For able readers